This Book
Belongs To

Eva x ....

For Susan, Home is where you are x
Special thanks to all at The Flat Cat Gallery, also to Caroline Jaquet,
Dave Gray and Paul Croan   AW

Thanks to Alan and Susan for all of your support, to my family for your
encouragement and to my canine inspiration Badger CH-H

Published by Little Door Books 2016
This edition published 2016

ISBN: 978-0-9927520-2-6

Text copyright   Alan Windram 2016
Illustrations copyright   Chloë Holwill-Hunter 2016

A CIP catalogue record for this book is available from the British Library.

Little Door Books

mail@littledoorbooks.co.uk
www.littledoorbooks.co.uk

Printed in China

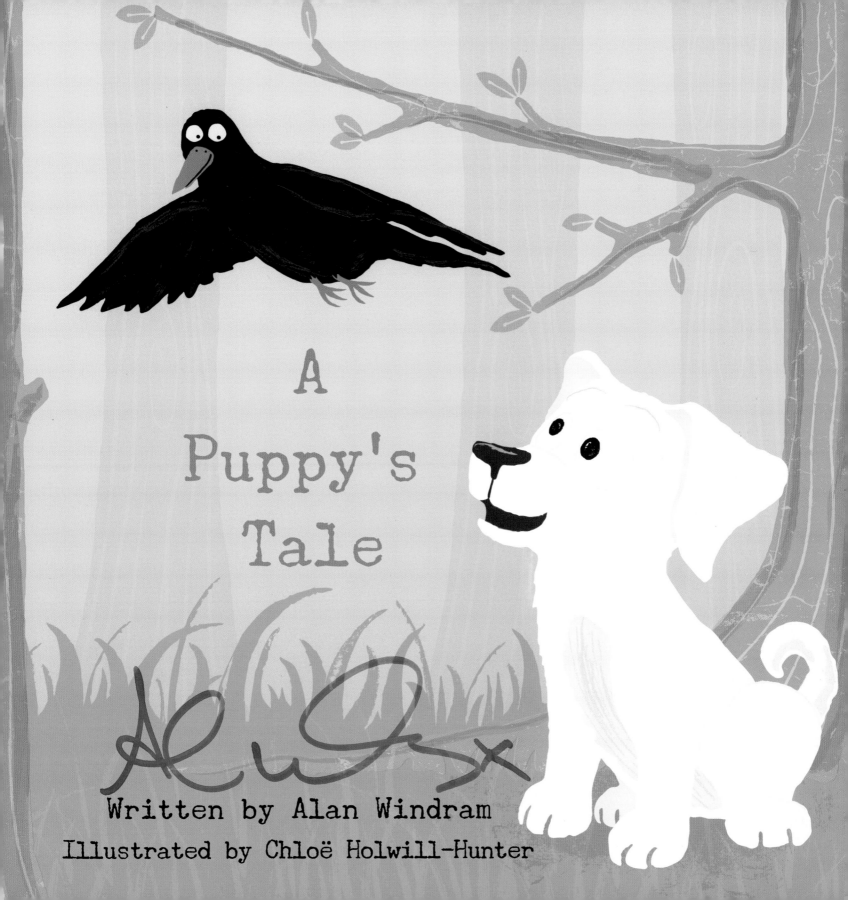

A Puppy's Tale

Written by Alan Windram

Illustrated by Chloë Holwill-Hunter

'Georgie! Georgie!!
Come on, we're going to be late,'
shouted mum.

But Georgie was always the last one home,
coming in after all the other puppies.

There were so many exciting things to see and smell
on the path.

JUMP.

jump.

jump.

Just then a little green frog bounced in front of Georgie and off into the tall grass.

'Wait for me, I want to play,' yelped Georgie as she scampered off the path after the little green frog.

jump, jump, jump.

'I wish I could jump like you,'
said Georgie.

But she couldn't jump as
high or as far as the
frog.

'Where are you going?'
asked Georgie.

'I'm going home,'
said the little green frog.

And all of a sudden the frog plopped into a
large pond, then was gone.

Out of the long grass hopped the happiest bunny rabbit Georgie had ever seen.

Hop, hop, hop.

'Wait for me, I want to play,' cried Georgie as she tried to hop like the hippity hoppity bunny, over the grass and into the wood.

'I wish I could hop like you,' said Georgie.

But she couldn't hop like the little bunny.

'Where are you going?'
asked Georgie.

'Yippee, I'm going home,'
said the bunny.

And with that, the happy little bunny wiggled its fluffy
white tail and disappeared down a hole in the ground.

A bushy-tailed red squirrel was picking up nuts under a very tall tree, running around so fast, scuttling and sniffing as it ran.

'Wait for me, I want to play,' pleaded Georgie, as she tried to catch up with the squirrel.

But it was too fast.

Georgie started to feel so dizzy and tired she flopped onto the ground.

The squirrel scampered up the tree with some juicy nuts in its mouth.

'Where are you going?'
asked Georgie.

'I'm going home for tea,'
said the bushy-tailed
squirrel.

Then it ran into a big
hole in the tree.

By this time
Georgie realised
she was so far
from the path
she was lost.

She sat down on the ground and started to cry.

High up in the branches of the very tall tree, a blackbird looked down at Georgie.

'What's wrong little puppy, why are you crying?' asked the blackbird.

'I'm tired, I'm hungry and now I'm lost,' said Georgie.

The blackbird just smiled and said:
'Don't worry little puppy, I will fly over
the wood and the fields, and help you
find your way back home.'

'Thank you so much,'
said Georgie.

So with the blackbird flying overhead, she led Georgie

out of the wood,

across the field, past the pond,

onto the path, and all the way home.

The End